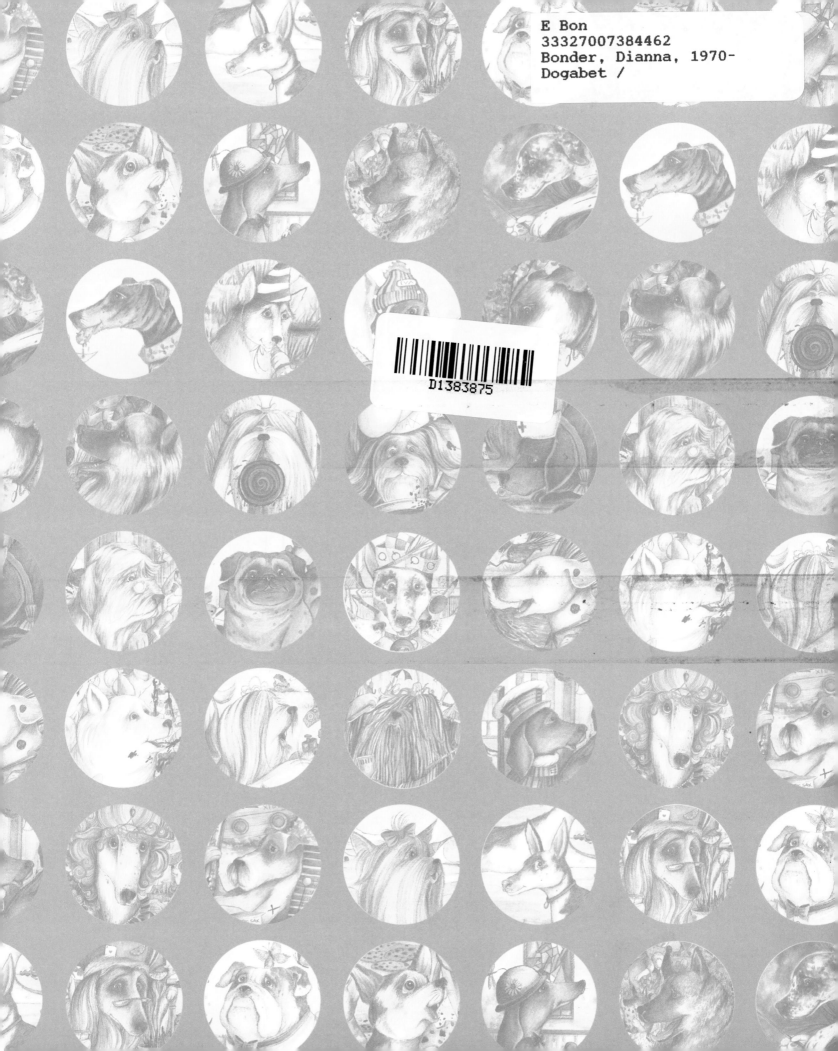

DOGABET

Dianna
Bonder

WALRUS
BOOKS

Aristocratic Afghan Hounds
attend abstract art auctions.

British Bulldogs balance
brilliant blue butterflies.

Chubby Chihuahuas cheerfully chew chocolate chip cookies.

Dapper Dachshunds daintily dunk delectable donuts.

Exuberant Elkhounds eagerly eat eighty exotic Easter eggs.

Frisky Foxhounds fish for fluttering fireflies.

Gluttonous Greyhounds greedily gulp gigantic green gherkins.

Hilarious Huskies honk huge harmonious horns.

Intelligent Irish Wolfhounds
interpret intricate ideograms.

Jolly Jack Russells joyfully jump jack-o'-lanterns.

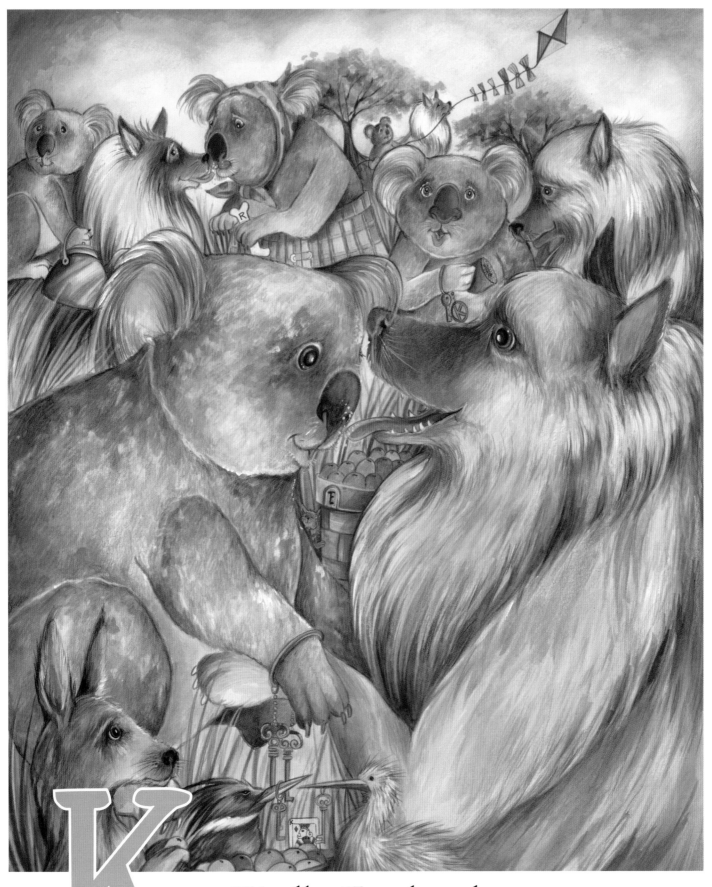

K

Kindly Keeshonds
kiss king-sized koalas.

Lovable Lhasa Apsos
lick large licorice lollipops.

M Many mischievous Mutts make marvelous mud muffins.

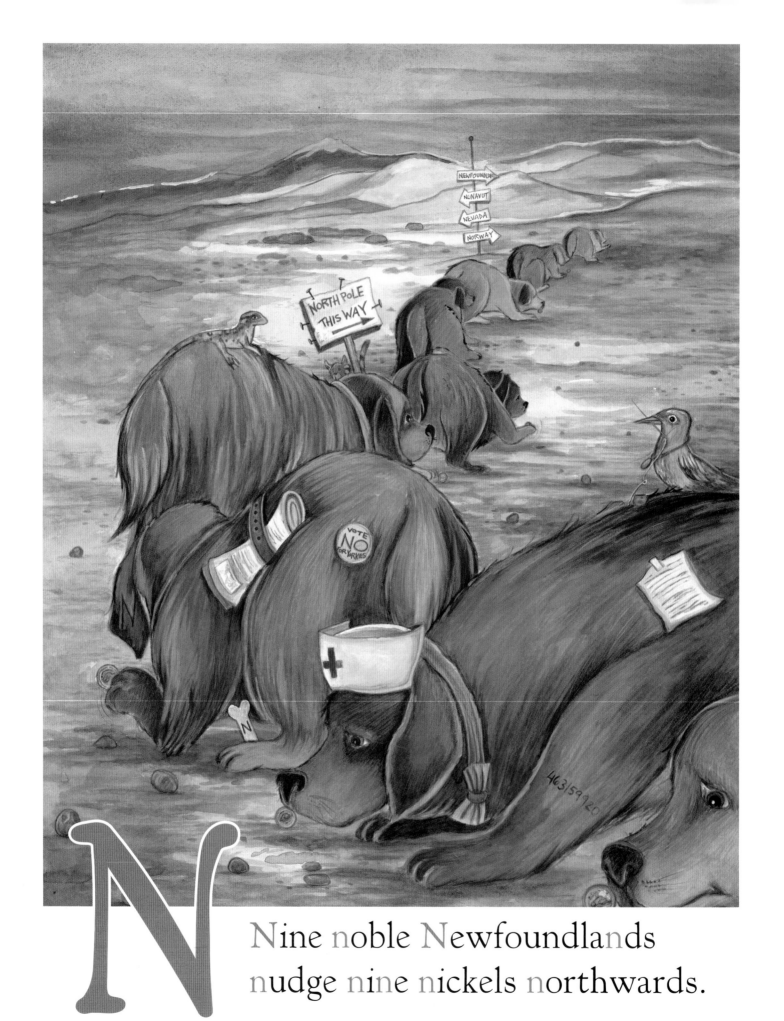

N Nine noble Newfoundlands
nudge nine nickels northwards.

Obedient Otterhounds
oil orange oaken oboes.

Perky pink Pugs play
purple pianos perfectly.

Quadruplet Queensland Heelers
quote quirky quotations quickly.

R Rambunctious Retrievers race raucous red roosters.

Seven silvery Samoyeds
sip sweet sticky syrup.

Twelve Tibetan Terriers toss
tiny toy trains.

U Unusual Pulis use useless
utensils uniquely.

Vivacious Vizslas vocalize
Victorian verses vividly.

Witty white Whippets
wear wild wispy wigs.

Six Fox Terriers wax
six exotic saxophones.

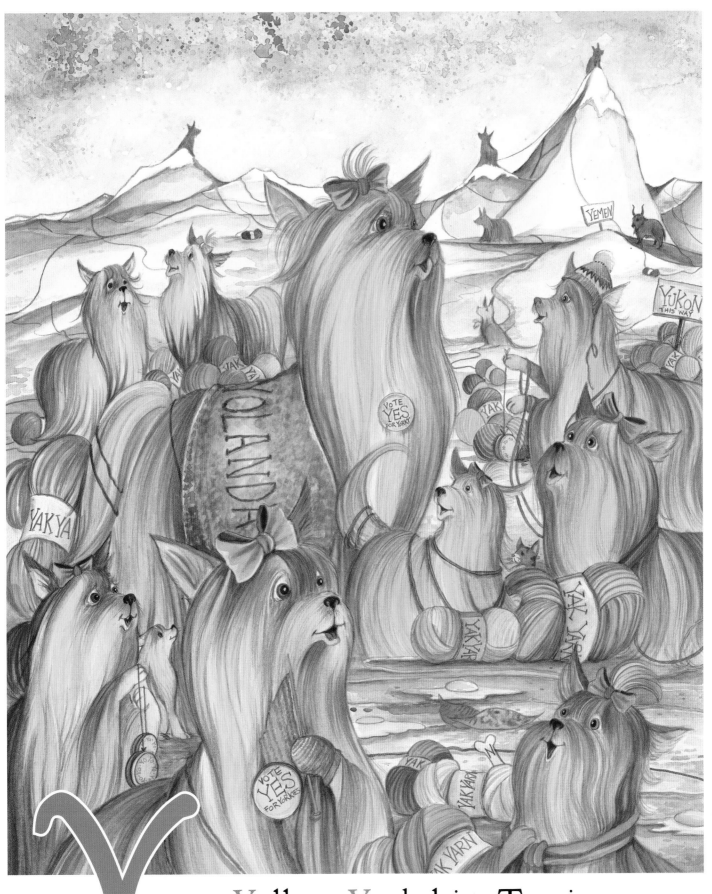

Yellow Yorkshire Terriers
yodel, yip and yowl.

Z Zany Ibizan Hounds
zig, zag and zip zealously.

Did you find all the hidden objects? Turn the page to see.

Find the hidden letter, cat and bone on each page. What else can you find?

Don't forget to put together the letters written on each hidden bone to figure out the hidden message.

 Aa

CAN YOU FIND?—Afghan Hounds: avocado, apple, apricot, asparagus, artwork, ace of hearts, armadillo, abstract art. HIDDEN LETTER—on the armadillo's back. HIDDEN CAT—sitting in the hallway towards the back archway. HIDDEN BONE—inside the painting on the wall to the far right.

Bb

CAN YOU FIND?—British Bulldogs: berries, bubbles, butterflies, beetle, book, bowl, brocolli, banana, bagel, boot, balloons, hot air balloon, buttons, bowtie, bandaid, bumblebee, ball, bucket, bat, buckle, bone, beads, bookmark. HIDDEN LETTER—the branch in the berry bushes forms a B. HIDDEN CAT—sitting behind the leg of the bulldog with the red bow tie. HIDDEN BONE—lying in front of the bulldog with a boot on its foot.

Cc

CAN YOU FIND?—Chihuahuas: cookies, Canadian flag, chocolate chips, cup, cat, compass, clock, can, corn, candle, carrots, canoe, crow, crayons, cookie jar, camel. HIDDEN LETTER—just beneath the can of corn the letter C is drawn with chocolate chips. HIDDEN CAT—sitting just beneath the pole of the hammock on the right-hand side. HIDDEN BONE—on the ground just above the back of the chihuahua carrying the large stack of cookies.

Dd

CAN YOU FIND?—Daschunds: dominos, donuts, daisy, diamonds, dragon, drum, dinosaur, dice, dragonfly, dress, dustpan, dove, dolphin, donkey, dartboard, darts, door, doorknob, derby hat. HIDDEN LETTER—inside the biggest donut (near the dog's paw). HIDDEN CAT—sleeping underneath the tablecloth. HIDDEN BONE—inside the pillow pattern.

Ee

CAN YOU FIND?—Elkhounds: eggs, emeralds, eye, ear, easter bunny, elephant, emu. HIDDEN LETTER—in the weaving of the basket. HIDDEN CAT—sitting beside basket of eggs just below the emu. HIDDEN BONE—inside the basket of eggs beside the cat.

Ff

CAN YOU FIND?—Foxhounds: frog, ferns, flamingo, flowers, fireflies, freckles, fishing rod. HIDDEN LETTER—in the fence in the far background. HIDDEN CAT—beside the flamingo. HIDDEN BONE—behind the rock beside the standing foxhound.

 Gg

CAN YOU FIND?—Greyhounds: goldfish, golf ball, grapefruit, gherkins, geese, garden gnome, garden, grass, grouse, glasses, grapes, grey clouds. HIDDEN LETTER—in the jar of pickles with the goldfish. HIDDEN CAT—sitting against a pickle in front of the grouse. HIDDEN BONE—The grey greyhound is holding it in his hand.

 Hh

CAN YOU FIND?—Huskies: hats, horns, halo, hummingbird, holly, heel sign, house, happy face, hedgehog, harmonica, hippopotamus. HIDDEN LETTER—inside the gold-coloured horn held by the Husky with the green and gold-striped hat. HIDDEN CAT—sitting beside the heel sign. HIDDEN BONE—at the base of the horn, which is being blown by the Husky with the polka dot hat.

 Ii

CAN YOU FIND?—Irish Wolfhounds: ice, igloo, iguana, ideogram, iron, icicles, ink, icebergs. HIDDEN LETTER—inside the igloo in the far right background. HIDDEN CAT—sitting in the igloo beside the snowman. HIDDEN BONE—in the foreground beside the dug up bone. ANSWER TO THE IDEOGRAM—Dogs are man's best friend.

 Jj

CAN YOU FIND?—Jack Russel dogs: jack-o'-lanterns, jellybeans, jack-in-the-box, jewellery, Jupiter, jigsaw puzzle pieces, jacket. HIDDEN LETTER—on the front of the jack in a box. HIDDEN CAT—hiding behind the tree. HIDDEN BONE—in the tree branches.

 Kk

CAN YOU FIND?—Keeshonds: kite, koalas, kiwi fruit, kiwi bird, keys, kingfisher bird, kangaroo, kerchief, kilt, kettle, king of diamonds. HIDDEN LETTER—on the keychain around the wrist of the koala holding the kiwi fruit. HIDDEN CAT—hiding behind the basket of kiwi fruit. HIDDEN BONE—in the hand of the koala with the kerchief.

Ll

CAN YOU FIND?—Lhasa Apsos: limes, lamps, ladybug, lentils, lemons, lemur, licorice lollipops, lightbulbs, lily, leopard, lava lamp, lobster, lace, leaves. HIDDEN LETTER—in the base of the lamp in the front. HIDDEN CAT—hiding behind the lobster. HIDDEN BONE—in the dog food bowl.

 Mm

CAN YOU FIND?—Mutts: mixing bowls, mud mix, muffin pan, money, measuring spoons, muffins, marmalade, milk, menu, measuring cup, monkey, mouse, mushrooms, mess, mitten. HIDDEN LETTER—in the wing of the blackish/grey rooster, close to the golden retriever's chin. HIDDEN CAT—sitting behind the leg of the blackish/grey rooster. HIDDEN BONE—beside the foot of the long-haired retriever.

N n

CAN YOU FIND?—Newfoundlands: nurse hat, note, numbers, nickels, necktie, newt, nightingale, North Pole sign, Norway sign, Nunavut sign, Newfoundland sign, Nevada sign, nuts, nose, nighttime. HIDDEN LETTER—in the fur of the big blue dog (around his neck area, close to the red bowl). HIDDEN CAT—licking stuff off the floor in the background. HIDDEN BONE—behind the red mixing bowl

O o

CAN YOU FIND?—Otterhounds: oranges, onion, otter, olives, oboes, oil, octopus, oar, office sign, October, opossum, owl, ostrich, oyster, ocean, oilcloth. HIDDEN LETTER—the optical lense, the blind pull cord. HIDDEN CAT—sitting behind the front-most dog's arm. HIDDEN BONE—in the otter's hand.

P p

CAN YOU FIND?—Pugs: peaches, popcorn, peas, pennies, pot, pumpkin, penguin, pickles, pearls, price tag, pizza, pear, porcupine, pigeon, parrot, pinata, painting, pedestal, perfume, plant, plug, popsicle, pianos, pie. HIDDEN LETTER—in the microphone. HIDDEN CAT—sitting behind the popcorn bowl. HIDDEN BONE—inside the popcorn machine.

Q q

CAN YOU FIND?—Queensland Heelers: quarters, quiz, quotations, quill, quiet sign, queen, quail, quack. HIDDEN LETTER—there are "Qs" all over the place . . . many to choose from. HIDDEN CAT—sitting behind the microphone. HIDDEN BONE—on the floor beside the quarters.

R r

CAN YOU FIND?—Retrievers: raspberries, rooster, roses, rhinoceros, reindeer, rattlesnake, rottweiler, rabbits, raven, raccoon, ribbon, red. HIDDEN LETTER—in the chocolate sauce on the vanilla ice cream on the sundae on the table. HIDDEN CAT—sitting way in the background. HIDDEN BONE—lying beside the Samoyed with the sock on his foot.

S s

CAN YOU FIND?—Samoyeds: spaghetti, strawberries, spoon, sugar cubes, soda, straw, sundaes, syrup, soup, snowballs, sock, sunflower, sun, sailboat, shrubs, seal, snake. HIDDEN LETTER—in the feather on the dog with the hat. HIDDEN CAT—sleeping behind the plant on the table. HIDDEN BONE—lying close to the viper snake.

T t

CAN YOU FIND?—Tibetan Terriers: trains, turtle, turkey, tulips, trees, toilet, trumpet, toque, tire swing, triangles, tiara, tongue, tu tu, traffic light. HIDDEN LETTER—in the small grey coal cart that the dog is juggling. HIDDEN CAT—sitting behind the turkey. HIDDEN BONE—behind the toad.

U u

CAN YOU FIND?—pUlis: underwear, utensils, umbrellas, UFOs, unicorn, ukulele. HIDDEN LETTER—lying in the grass just above the underwear to the far right. HIDDEN CAT—sitting inside the upside-down umbrella. HIDDEN BONE—in the tangles of the puli's hair.

V v

CAN YOU FIND?—Vislas: violets, vulture, viper, valentine card, violin, vinegar, volcano, veil. HIDDEN LETTER—in the feather on the dog with the hat. HIDDEN CAT—sleeping behind the plant on the table. HIDDEN BONE—close to the viper snake.

W w

CAN YOU FIND?—Whippets: watermelon, wigs, wren, wristwatch, wasps, wig pins, web, water fountain. HIDDEN LETTER—in the spider web. HIDDEN CAT—behind the watermelon to the far left. HIDDEN BONE—in the hand of the purple-haired whippet.

X x

CAN YOU FIND?—Fox Terriers: xylophone, quiz with the X marks, X's and O's game sheet in the water, X marks the spot on the map. HIDDEN LETTERS—tattoo on the arm of the dog in the inflatable tube, on the map, on the sails, on the quiz, on the X and O game sheet, the no fishing sign, the no exit sign. HIDDEN CAT—sitting on the floating can of wax. HIDDEN BONE—in the boat just above the map.

Y y

CAN YOU FIND?—Yorkshire Terriers: yarn, yorkies, yams, yolks, Yukon sign, Yemen sign, yak, vote "yes" badges, yo-yos. HIDDEN LETTER—on the side of the tallest mountain (although there are Y's in lots of the words as well). HIDDEN CAT—sitting behind the ball of yarn beside the the two yorkies standing on the far right-hand side. HIDDEN BONE—just below the yams.

Z z

CAN YOU FIND?—Ibizan Hounds: zucchini, zinnias, zucchini, Zeppelin, zebras, Zeus. HIDDEN LETTER—in the bum of the viszla with the blue collar, leaping across the page. HIDDEN CAT—sitting behind the zucchini by the sign "Zack's Zucchini." HIDDEN BONE—behind the leaves just above "Zack's Zucchini."

I dedicate this book to the wonderful Gabriola Island moms, who have helped and supported me throughout the process of creating
this book—from hosting play dates for my daughter Ekko, when I needed time to work, to cheering me on to the finish.
To Twin Cedars Veterinary Clinic for all the wonderful dog books and reference materials.
To my husband and daughter for their continued patience.
To Big Heart Rescue for the very special work they do and for bringing our new dog Sara into our lives.
To Noah's Wish for all their difficult work through disasters and for caring for our lost family members.
And finally to all the dogs in my life, past and present. Without them, I wouldn't know the meaning of devotion.
Thank you, everyone!

Copyright © 2007 by Dianna Bonder
Walrus Books, an imprint of Whitecap Books

Edited by Lesley Cameron
Proofread by Ben D'Andrea
Cover design by Five Seventeen
Book design by Michelle Mayne
Typeset by Jesse Marchand

Printed and bound in Hong Kong

LIBRARY AND ARCHIVES CANADA CATALOGUING
IN PUBLICATION

Bonder, Dianna, 1970–
      Dogabet / Dianna Bonder, author and illustrator.

ISBN 1-55285-797-2
ISBN 978-1-55285-797-7

      1. English language—Alphabet—Juvenile literature.
      2. Alphabet books.
      3. Dogs—Juvenile literature. I. Title.

PE1155.B66 2006   j421'.1   C2006-902283-6

The publisher acknowledges the financial support of the Canada Council for the Arts, the British Columbia Arts Council, and the Government of Canada through the Book Publishing
Industry Development Program (BPIDP). Whitecap Books also acknowledges the financial support of the Province of British Columbia through the Book Publishing Tax Credit.

Dianna Bonder is donating a portion of her royalties from Dogabet to Noah's Wish (USA)—Animal Disaster Rescue, involved with the relief effort following Hurricane Katrina—and Big
Heart Rescue Society (Canada)—Dog Rescue Society dedicated to improving the lives of homeless, abused, or neglected pets.